IT'S COOL
TO BE
KIND

IT'S COOL TO BE KIND

By

Linnea McFadden

Illustrated by

Ayanami Monreal

Linnea McFadden
P.O. Box 167
96 Commerce Drive
Wyomissing, PA 19610

www.linneamcfadden.com

Publisher's Note: This is a work of fiction. Names, characters, places, and incidents are a product of the author's imagination. Locales and public names are sometimes used for atmospheric purposes. Any resemblance to actual people, living or dead, or to businesses, companies, events, institutions, or locales is completely coincidental.

Book design © 2013, BookDesignTemplates.com

Illustrations and Book Cover Design by Ayanami Monreal
Edited by Beth Levan

Ordering Information: Special discounts are available on quantity purchases by corporations, associations, and others. For details, contact the publisher at the address above.

It's Cool to Be Kind / Linnea McFadden — First Edition

ISBN 978-0-9984681-0-5

Printed in the United States of America

To Hanna, Tommy and Tom.

Thank you for bringing such joy to my life.

Chapter

1

It was just a few weeks into the new school year at Rock Hill Elementary, and so far, everything was going great for Beckett Barnes. There was a chill in the air every morning, and the days were flying by. He wouldn't admit it to his friends, but Beckett enjoyed going to school. His favorite parts were playing scooter tag at gym and wall ball at recess.

Before school started, he'd been so pumped when he found out that not only did he get the fourth-grade teacher everyone wanted (Mr. Williams) but also that his best friends Tony and Dan were going to be in his class. How could the year go wrong with all that awesomeness? Plus, this year, they were learning how to code video games on the computer. So cool! Even after school started, he didn't mind that Mr. Williams called on him almost every day to come up to explain a math problem to the rest of the class.

Beckett had been best buds with Tony and Dan since kindergarten. On the first day of school that year, a boy with red hair and freckles walked into the classroom with his hands in the air saying loudly, "Wassup? Class can start now. Tony is here!"

Then, at recess that day, Tony had taken out a deck of cards.

"Pick a card! Any card! And I will know what card you picked," Tony had chanted loudly.

"Okay, I'm in," Beckett answered, curious to see if the magic trick would really work. He then picked a 10 of hearts and put it back in the deck. Tony shuffled the cards and pulled out the 10 of hearts.

"Is this your card? Wait, what's your name dude?" Tony had asked.

"Beckett. And yes, that is my card! How did you DO that?" Beckett was shocked that Tony had actually picked his card.

"A magician never shows his tricks," Tony had grinned. After that, they had become fast friends. Tony ended up showing his easier tricks to Beckett but kept the best for himself. He was constantly pulling pranks or telling jokes from the joke book he carried around in his pocket.

Kids still talked about the prank Tony pulled on the last day of school in third grade. At the end of the day, he'd excused himself and gone to the bathroom. When the bell rang, he opened up a can of confetti in the middle of the hallway and then ran back to his classroom. The students who saw it had laughed and ran through the halls trying to catch the red and white papers flying through the air as they left school.

The principal, on the other hand, had not been so happy. She'd made Tony stay late and vacuum up every single piece of confetti. She'd said it wasn't fair for the custodian to have to clean up Tony's mess. His parents had agreed; they were furious with him for causing such chaos at school. When Tony's dad picked him up that afternoon, his face had been even redder than Tony's hair, and he yelled, "TONY!! WHAT DID YOU DO??"

Tony was lucky his only punishment was to be grounded for two weeks. He'd said that he didn't mind being grounded. He'd collected some of the confetti and put it in a glass jar on his dresser to remind him of that day.

Dan didn't start kindergarten until the middle of the year. The day he arrived, he had walked into the classroom with his head down and his eyes peering out of his long black bangs. He wouldn't look at anyone and quickly slid into his chair. When the teacher asked him to tell the class his name and a few things about himself, he'd hid behind his folder and answered so softly that the rest of the class had to lean closer straining to hear him.

"My name is Dan. My parents were born in China but moved to Philadelphia before I was born. We just moved here last week."

Every day, Beckett tried talking to him. But it had taken three weeks before Dan would even respond. Beckett finally had luck when he'd asked, "What is your favorite football team?"

"The Philadelphia Eagles. I really hope they win the Super Bowl sometime!" Dan had answered with a smile.

Dan absolutely loved sports, especially football. He was extremely fast and would surprise the other team with his speed. He always had football cards with him and wore his Darren Sproles #43 jersey every chance he got.

Beckett stood out in a crowd because of his bright white blond hair. He had been at Rock Hill Elementary ever since kindergarten and knew almost every kid at school; he even made a point of getting to know the younger kids. The kids also knew who Beckett was because he made the best trick shots. At the beginning of the year, he'd thrown a ball onto the school roof during recess. It had bounced off and swished right into the basketball net!

Beckett had yelled, "Now that is called the Roof Shot!"

It was so amazing that it could have been on Dude Perfect! All the kids who'd been at recess that day had cheered and high fived Beckett. Tony even got the kids chanting "Beckett! Beckett! Beckett!"

Yes, Beckett had been loving fourth grade. Then one day, out of the blue, something changed. He had been saying hi to kids in the hallways like he usually did when he noticed that many of the other kids looked nervous. Beckett wondered what was going on. Then he noticed a new kid with dark curly hair walking down the hall. Beckett said hello to him, but the kid just glared back with a scowl before giving Beckett a shove with his shoulder. Beckett was shocked. The kid muttered "Loser" as he walked by.

Later that day, during a break in class, Beckett asked Tony and Dan, "Did you guys see the new kid?" He didn't tell them about the shove. Who knows, he thought to himself, maybe the kid is just having a bad day.

"Dude, I heard that he punched two kids in the arm!" Tony exclaimed.

"When I was walking down to the nurse, I saw him push a kid in the stairwell. Luckily the kid didn't fall down the stairs! But I was too nervous to say anything to him. He looks like he could really hurt someone," Dan added.

Beckett wasn't surprised to hear this news. He was relieved when he didn't run into the new kid again.

After school, Beckett yelled out to Tony and Dan, "See you on the field for football!"

Tony yelled back, "Can't wait! Today's the day that our team totally creams your team!!"

"Yeah, right – I'd love to see that happen!" Beckett teased. He loved playing two-hand touch with his friends after school, especially Tony because he didn't play on the football team. Tony just came out for the games after school and talked smack the entire time cracking everyone up.

The game was a close one – 14 to 14. On the last play of the game, the quarterback on Beckett's team threw the ball to him. It whizzed over his head, but Beckett was determined to get it. He jumped for the ball, grabbed it out of the air with one hand and dove into the end zone. As he hit the ground, he put his hand up in the air with the football in it. His team went wild! Beckett had scored a touchdown with a one-handed catch just like Odell Beckham Jr. of the New York Giants. They won the game! What made it even better was that Beckett was wearing his Beckham Jr. jersey that day!

"DUDE!!! I don't even mind losing to you because that was so awesome!" Tony hollered. He jumped in the air and chest bumped Beckett.

Chapter

2

Over the next few days, the whole school was buzzing about the new kid. His name was Porter Reed. He was in the fifth grade, and rumor had it that he would trip kids for no reason and punch kids as he passed them in the halls. But all of the kids were so scared of him that no one had the guts to tell a teacher!

Beckett had not seen Porter in action until one day when he was on the way to the office. He saw Porter purposely block a first-grade boy who was holding a bathroom pass and not let the boy by.

"Kid, you are such a baby," Porter smirked at the first grader.

"Leave him alone!" Beckett said loudly, so angry that Porter was picking on a kid so much smaller than him.

Porter's eyes widened. Clenching his fists, he pushed Beckett. "Don't mess with me, kid. You have no idea what I will do to you." He glared at the first grader as he walked away.

"Are you okay?" Beckett asked the first grader, who was shaking and crying. The boy nodded, but it took a while before he calmed down.

"That Porter is not a nice guy. Just stay away from him," Beckett warned. When the boy stopped crying, Beckett walked him back to his class and told the teacher what had happened.

The next day, Tony and Dan came running up to Beckett when he got to school.

"DUDE!! Did you hear that Porter is planning to knock you out for telling on him?" Tony yelled.

"No," Beckett said with his heart racing and his palms sweating. He knew he didn't stand a chance against Porter. He had never fought anyone in his life!

"There's no way he'd try to beat me up. I bet he's just bluffing," Beckett said acting like it was no big deal. But Tony and Dan saw right through his act.

"Beckett, I don't blame you if you're scared. I'd be petrified!" Dan said.

"Yeah, dude, he'd totally demolish you!" Tony snorted.

"Thanks for your encouragement, Tony," Beckett said laughing. He decided he would have to avoid Porter so he wouldn't get knocked out.

"Can you guys help me steer clear of Porter?" Beckett asked.

"No problem," Tony answered quickly, but Dan hesitated.

"As long as I don't have to go anywhere near him," Dan replied.

Once the news spread that Porter was getting detention for what he'd done to the first grader, all of the kids at school became lookouts for Beckett. As kids were walking to lunch or specials with their classes, they would whisper to him as his class walked by, "Porter is walking down the stairs" or "Porter's class is headed this way!"

Beckett would thank them and then duck down behind a bunch of his classmates until Porter's class passed. One afternoon, Beckett was pumped for football with his friends after school when he noticed Porter standing outside the doorway to the field behind the school. Tony came running up and said, "Beckett! Porter found out you play football after school without any adults around and is waiting to beat you up."

Beckett's heart sank. Now he wouldn't be able to play football after school either. This went on for weeks. It was exhausting hiding from Porter, and he really missed playing football with his buddies.

Every morning, Beckett woke up with a pit in his stomach worrying about getting beat up by Porter. He noticed that he was even starting to NOT like going to school.

Chapter

3

One night after football practice, Beckett was playing soccer in the backyard with his older brother, Benji, before dinner. Beckett idolized Benji because he was good at *everything*. His parents loved telling the story about how when Beckett was a baby and could finally sit up, Benji had put a ball in his hand expecting Beckett to throw it back to him. Luckily for Benji, Beckett loved sports as much as he did. Benji was now in seventh grade and had taught Beckett how to play baseball, soccer, football, lacrosse and basketball. Benji was amazing at soccer. No one could ever get the ball from him.

But the main reason that Beckett looked up to Benji was because of how nice he was to everyone. He always did what he could to help people. He was president of his class and had started a charity to help kids with cancer. He'd even organized a race that raised a ton of money for the charity.

During their game, Beckett tried his hardest to get the ball from Benji. Each time his brother blew past him, Beckett's anger and frustration over all that had been happening the past few weeks grew until it finally bubbled over. He purposely slide tackled Benji, kicking him hard in the shin as he took him down.

Benji was furious because he knew that it was a cheap shot and that Beckett wasn't going for the ball. He lunged over and knocked Beckett to the ground. They started wrestling and punching each other as hard as they could.

Their mom was in the kitchen and saw what was happening through the window. She yelled out, "Absolutely not, boys! You know better than to fight like that. Stop it!" She could tell this was more than horse play and was getting out of hand, and she wouldn't stand for it.

"Dude, what was that for?!" Benji yelled at Beckett.

"You are no fun to play with Benji! You never let me get the ball!" Beckett screamed back at him.

"I can't help that you stink at soccer Beckett!" Benji yelled. Beckett shoved Benji as hard as he could. They started wrestling again.

Just as they were arguing in the backyard, their dad came home. He was surprised by all the commotion. Dad didn't let Benji and Beckett fight, and he was very strict.

The boys looked at him nervously. They were worried that they were going to be in trouble. But Dad could tell something serious was going on.

"We will talk about it at dinner," Dad decided. Benji and Beckett looked at each other with raised eyebrows. They knew they were about to be in big trouble.

During a delicious dinner of spaghetti and meatballs – Beckett's favorite – Dad looked at Benji and asked, "So what just happened?"

"It was all Beckett's fault, Dad. You should've seen how he slide tackled me. He wasn't going for the ball and just kicked me as hard as he could in the shins," Benji responded angrily.

"And then what did you do, Benji?" Dad asked.

"I tackled him and punched him. But he started it!" Benji replied.

"I don't care what Beckett did first. You know you aren't supposed to punch him. You are both grounded from the X-box for two weeks!" said

Dad. Benji glared at Beckett. He didn't think the punishment was fair since it was all Beckett's fault.

"Beckett, what do you have to say for yourself?" Dad asked.

"It's not my fault, Dad! He's no fun to play with because he never lets me get the ball," Beckett complained.

"But why would you purposely hurt your brother? You know how much it hurts to get kicked in the shins. You would be mad if he did that to you," Dad asked.

Beckett was annoyed. His dad was a counselor, and sometimes, he used his counseling techniques on them. Beckett was definitely not in the mood for that right now. Plus, he just didn't want to talk about what was happening with Porter. It was embarrassing. He looked down and wouldn't answer. He knew it was making his dad mad, but he didn't care.

Mom looked at Beckett and said, "Beckett, you've been playing soccer with your brother for years. Sometimes you get frustrated when you can't get the ball from him, but you've never acted like this. Something else is going on. What is it?"

Beckett shrugged and looked down. His insides were going crazy. He didn't want to talk about Porter and was racking his brain to find a way to get out of this conversation.

"We can't help you if you don't tell us," Dad said while leaning over and rubbing Beckett's shoulder.

Beckett looked up and saw that Dad and Mom looked really worried. As much as he didn't want to talk about Porter, maybe he would feel better if he told them.

"Fine! I'll tell you," Beckett said. "There's this new kid at school – Porter. He's such a jerk and is mean to all of the kids. A few weeks ago, I saw him being mean to a first grader, and I told him to stop. Porter told me not to mess with him, but I told the first grader's teacher what happened and Porter got in trouble. After that, Porter told everyone he was going to knock me out."

"Who does this kid think he is? I'll go to the school and beat him up myself!" Benji yelled. Dad and Mom both looked at Benji shaking their heads.

"What? No one messes with my brother!" Benji said defiantly.

"Benji, I'm happy to hear that you want to help your brother. But you shouldn't ever hit anyone, and you should NEVER beat anyone up," Mom said looking at Benji sternly.

Dad passed the meatballs to Beckett and asked, "What did you do when you heard that Porter was going to knock you out?"

As he filled his plate with meatballs, Beckett said, "I've been hiding from him ever since. I have friends and other kids at school helping me by keeping an eye out for him. It's embarrassing having to hide behind my friends when we pass his class in the hall. And he even waits for me after school."

"Is that why you haven't been playing football with your friends after school?" asked Mom.

"Yes. I miss playing, especially with Tony because he is hilarious with his smack talk," Beckett answered.

"I can understand not wanting to confront Porter because you don't want to fight. But how long can you keep this up?" Dad asked.

Beckett didn't answer. The stress and worry showed in his face.

"Beckett, your reaction to this situation has been to run away. It sounds like that's getting tiring and making you unhappy. Remember the equation we always talk about? Event + Response = Outcome. You can change the outcome of this situation by choosing a different response. What's my favorite story about this?" Dad asked.

"I remember the story. It was when we went away a couple of years ago with Aunt Maureen and her family. We all met at the Outer Banks and stayed where you had to drive on the beach for 10 miles to get to our house. We had so much fun in our car with the windows open, blasting the music and dancing, while in the other car, Aunt Maureen was crying on the floor about how scared she was that her car was going to get stuck in the sand," said Beckett. They all laughed remembering how Aunt Maureen had fallen out of her car when they got to the house, screaming about how awful that car ride had been.

"I love that example of how there is more than one way to respond to the exact same situation. It shows how much the response changes the outcome. We were happy, and Aunt Maureen was miserable. Beckett, you are the one who is miserable now. You can't keep running away from this kid. You need to find a different response," said Dad.

"DAD!! I can't confront this kid!!! He will annihilate me! You haven't seen how big he is or how MEAN he is!" Beckett shrieked.

Benji interrupted, "Dad — just let me go to the school and at least intimidate this bully so he leaves Beckett alone!"

"Benji, would that really help Beckett learn to stand up for himself?" asked Dad.

"No, Dad, but I'm so mad!" Benji said. Beckett looked over at Benji and smiled, happy that he wanted to protect him.

"Benji, thanks for wanting to help. I wish you could. I shouldn't have slide tackled and hit you. I'm sorry," said Beckett.

Benji grinned, playfully punched Beckett's arm and said, "Only I am allowed to beat up on you!"

Mom smiled, "Benji, I completely understand that you want to help your brother. I feel the same way. I want to do something too." She was very upset that a boy was being mean to her son. She wanted to call the principal and get this boy in trouble for his behavior, but she also wanted Beckett to learn to stand up for himself.

"Beckett, it sounds like you need to confront Porter. But it has to be in a safe environment where he can't hit you. Is there somewhere you could do that?" Mom asked.

Beckett thought about it for a moment. "I guess I could speak to him with an adult present. Maybe I could ask the guidance counselor, Mrs. Gables, to meet with the two of us. She's always been nice to me and part of her job is to help kids who are having problems."

Dad, Mom and Benji all agreed that this was a great plan. Beckett felt like a huge weight had been lifted off of him. Now, he had a plan that would hopefully help him avoid getting his lights knocked out!

That night, when Beckett's mom came in to say good night, they did their evening ritual of talking about his day and naming three things that he was grateful for. Beckett thought long and hard about it and finally said, "Okay, here goes. 1. I'm grateful that you, Dad and Benji helped me come up with a plan for how to handle the situation with Porter. I've been losing sleep over it and feeling miserable. 2. I'm grateful Benji didn't stay mad at me for slide tackling him. 3. I'm most grateful for the awesome dinner you made tonight!"

His mom smiled. "I'd like you to think about Porter and how he is feeling. You didn't act like yourself today when you slide tackled Benji. You behaved that way because you were upset about what was happening at school, and you took it out on your brother."

Beckett hadn't thought at all about how Porter felt. He just thought of Porter as a mean jerk who had no feelings.

"Mom, Porter has been so mean to everyone ever since the day he started school here. Maybe he's just a bully."

"Or maybe he didn't want to move here and is upset about it. You don't know what's going on in his life. Whatever is happening might be impacting how he's acting," Mom responded.

"Good point, Mom," said Beckett. "I'll think about that."

Beckett's mom gave him a kiss good night. "I'm proud of you, honey."

Chapter

4

Beckett woke up the next morning with a smile. He felt better than he had in weeks. When he arrived at school, he went straight to Mrs. Gables to ask about the meeting.

"Mrs. Gables, the new kid has threatened to beat me up for telling on him for being mean to a first grader," Beckett said.

"I'm glad you came and told me about this. You know that we have a no bullying policy at this school. I will speak with Porter this morning and then speak to both of your teachers to let them know that we will be meeting after lunch," said Mrs. Gables.

"Thank you," said Beckett as Mrs. Gables walked him to the door.

When it was time for the meeting, Beckett got up quickly and accidentally knocked over his chair. Tony whispered to him, "Good luck, Dude."

Beckett nodded and walked out of the room. On the way to the meeting, his stomach was in knots. What if Porter didn't care that an adult was in the room and just knocked him out anyway? Beckett started getting himself worked up and had to take numerous long deep breaths to calm himself down.

When he got to Mrs. Gables' office, Porter was already sitting in the waiting area. Beckett held his breath and sat down quickly without saying anything or making eye contact with Porter.

A few minutes later, Mrs. Gables came out and called the two boys into her office. She had them sit in a circle together, which meant that he was fortunately not within punching distance, a huge relief for Beckett.

"I've heard you two may have gotten off on the wrong foot. So I wanted to give you a chance to make things better," said Mrs. Gables.

Porter gave Beckett a death stare, but neither one of them said a word.

Beckett just stared at the floor. No one spoke for a few minutes. Mrs. Gables looked at Beckett and smiled. "Beckett, you can start now. I'm here, and it's going to be okay."

Beckett cleared his throat, and while still staring at the floor, he shakily said, "Well... like Mrs. Gables just said, we seem to have gotten off on the wrong foot. Maybe we can start over. My name is Beckett, and I am in the fourth grade. Where did you move here from?"

"I moved here from Michigan. I don't want to be here at all. My parents made me move because my dad was transferred here for work. I wanted to stay in Michigan. I was the quarterback for my football team. They're going to the championship, and now I won't be there to help them win. What's even worse is that we moved here too late for me to be able to play football. So I'm not doing anything. I hate it here. I hate the people. Everyone here is so annoying," Porter answered.

Beckett thought about how he would feel if he were in Porter's shoes. He couldn't imagine how upset he'd be if he wasn't able to play football on his team and had to miss a championship game. And not being able to play football at all was unimaginable! Beckett decided to help Porter.

"I play football, too," he said. "I'd be upset if I was in your situation. I don't blame you for being mad. What if I talk to my football coach and see if you can help out at practices either with the older teams or the younger flag football teams? I know it isn't as fun as actually playing, but it's better than nothing. At least this way, you could get a chance to get to know the coaches, which would help you next year when you try out. They may say no, but it's worth a try."

Porter looked shocked and asked, "You'd do that for me? Even after I threatened to knock you out?" As he said that, he looked at Mrs. Gables nervously. She just nodded for them to continue.

"I wasn't happy that you threatened to beat me up and waited for me after school. It made me miss weeks of football games with my friends. I was miserable," Beckett said.

Porter looked down sheepishly and said, "Man, I'm sorry I made you miss your football games after school. I bet you're mad at me."

"I was mad. But now that I understand why you were acting that way, I'm not mad anymore. But it doesn't make it okay how you treated me and other kids at school," Beckett responded. "Your response to moving here and treating people meanly made things so bad for you here."

"It's not my fault that I had to move here!" Porter said angrily.

"No. It's not your fault, but you could've acted differently. In my family, we talk about how our response to any situation can change the outcome. And you...," Beckett said.

Porter interrupted, "I don't understand how someone's response can change the outcome. Like my moving here. I couldn't control that at all!" He glared at Beckett.

Mrs. Gables joined in and said, "Porter, you had every right to be angry because your parents moved you here. But you could've responded differently to it."

"What else could I have done?" Porter said while still glaring at Beckett.

Beckett said, "What I mean is that you had a right to be upset. But you could've moved here and been nicer to kids at school. If you'd tried to make the best of the situation, you wouldn't be the most feared kid in school and have no friends."

"Seriously? Kids are that scared of me? I know I haven't been nice, but I didn't think I was that bad," Porter said with a surprised look on his face.

"Yeah, I think every kid at school is seriously scared of you. I certainly am – I mean, I was scared of you until today. Now I understand more about why you were acting that way."

"But what can I do to change it now that I'm stuck here and don't have any friends?" Porter asked. Beckett thought about it and came up with an idea.

"Why don't you come and play two-hand touch football with me and my friends after school today?" Beckett asked. As he was saying that out loud, in his head, he was hoping his friends wouldn't be mad at him for bringing the meanest kid Rock Hill Elementary had ever seen to their football game!

"Man! Really? That would be awesome," said Porter. "I miss playing football."

Mrs. Gables smiled and said, "I'm happy that you boys were able to work out your differences. Beckett, it's really nice of you to ask your coach if Porter can help. I'm glad that he'll be able to play football with your friends. Porter, you need to change your behavior. The way you've been acting is not permitted at this school. You'll need to make amends to the kids you've scared or hurt, starting with that first grader."

"I'll apologize and try to be nicer. But what if the kids don't care because I've been so mean?" Porter said.

"I'll tell them you aren't so bad," Beckett offered.

"Not so bad??" Porter laughed.

"Okay, boys, great job talking things through. If you have any other problems or concerns, don't hesitate to reach out to me again." Mrs. Gables was smiling as she walked them out of her office.

Chapter

5

When Beckett walked back into his class, Tony and Dan looked up anxiously. They were absolutely sure he was going to have a black eye after having been in the same room as Porter. Beckett smiled at their shocked faces and gave them a thumbs up.

As they walked out to recess, Tony asked, "Dude! What happened?"

"Porter hates it here. He's a quarterback, and his team is going to the championship game. He's mad that he is missing it," Beckett said.

"He didn't try to PUNCH you before you went into Mrs. Gables' office?" Dan asked. Beckett smiled and said, "I was worried about that when I got to her office and saw him sitting there."

"Dude! We were totally planning on taking turns visiting you in the hospital! I've been practicing my juggling routine so I could cheer you up while you were in there," Tony joked.

Beckett laughed, "You guys are the best!"

"So what happened at the meeting?" Dan asked.

"We talked about why he didn't like it here. I'd be mad too if I had to move and miss my championship game. He took his anger out on kids at school, which wasn't right. But he seemed sorry for how he's been acting."

Later that day, as Beckett, Tony and Dan were walking down the hall to their coding class, Porter's class was heading their way. Tony and Dan looked at each other uneasily, but when Porter passed Beckett, he gave him a fist bump, then nodded at Tony and Dan.

"Hey, Dudes," Porter said. Tony and Dan stopped in their tracks completely shocked. Porter smiled as he walked by.

"How could just one meeting with him change his behavior so much?" Dan asked completely confused.

"Oh! I almost forgot! I also asked him to play football with us after school," Beckett told them. Tony and Dan looked at each other with raised eyebrows and shrugged nervously.

After school that day at the football game, all of the boys looked scared when they saw Porter walk up.

"Why in the world is Porter here? Is he planning to beat us up?" one of Beckett's friends whispered nervously.

Beckett laughed, "No, he's actually surprisingly nice. He just got off on the wrong foot here and is trying to make his situation better. He loves football, and we can help him by making him feel included." The boys agreed to give it a chance, but they were doubtful and really thought one of them was going to end up injured.

During the game, Porter noticed that the boys loved making one-handed catches. He threw passes they had to dive for, and they all loved it! At the end of the game, all of the boys went up to Porter and told him what a great arm he had and that they loved playing with him. Beckett was really happy to see Porter beaming and high fiving everyone.

"Dude! You can really throw! I bet your football team is upset that they don't have you for the championship game," Tony shouted loudly while fist bumping Porter.

Porter smiled, "Thanks, man. I'm so bummed I'm missing it. I really enjoyed getting my hands on the football today. You guys sure are crazy with how you dive for any ball thrown at you. Made it a ton of fun for me."

Later that evening at football practice, Beckett approached Coach Taget.

"Hey, Coach, there's a new kid at school who really loves football. He had to move before he could help his team win the championship game this season. And he came too late to play football here. Do you think he could help out at practice? He played two-hand touch football with us after school today. You should see the arm he has!"

"I guess we could use an extra hand at practice, especially if he has a good arm. Let him know he can come," Coach Taget answered.

Chapter

6

That night at dinner, Beckett couldn't wait to tell his family about all that had happened.

"You were right about Porter, Mom. He didn't want to move here. His football team is going to the championship. Now that they live here, he won't be able to play in the game, and he's really angry about it. I felt bad for him so I asked him to play football with my friends after school."

"How did it go at football?" asked Mom.

"Most of my friends weren't happy about it at first, but once Porter started playing and they saw how well he could throw, they got over it. Plus, he was really nice to everyone!" answered Beckett.

Mom smiled. "I'm glad that you took the time to get to know Porter and see past his behavior and find out who he is as a person. It sounds like he really isn't so bad."

"Oh, I almost forgot. He's going to help out at football practice, too. I talked to Coach Taget today. I am introducing Porter to him tomorrow," Beckett beamed.

"That's great, Beckett," said Dad.

"Dude! I'm glad that you didn't get beat up by that kid! Proud of you for taking care of it yourself. But you know I could have kicked his butt!" Benji said.

"Benji!!" said Mom. They all cracked up laughing.

Later that night before bed, Beckett shared with his mom the three things he was grateful for that day. "1. I'm grateful my conversation with Porter went so well. 2. I'm grateful my friends were so accepting of Porter at football. They could've said he wasn't allowed to play. 3. I'm grateful to have such a supportive family." Mom smiled and kissed him goodnight.

Porter met Beckett before football practice the next day. Beckett and Porter walked over to Coach Taget.

"Coach, this is Porter, the kid I was telling you about," Beckett said.

"Nice to meet you, kid. I heard you have a great arm. Looking forward to seeing you throw," Coach Taget said as he shook Porter's hand.

"I'm excited to help out. I miss playing football. Thanks," Porter smiled broadly.

Chapter

7

Not all the kids at school were as accepting of Porter as Beckett's friends. It took some time, and Porter had to work hard to be nice to people. It did help when kids saw Beckett talking to Porter. But for the little kids, it was much harder. When Porter said hi, the younger kids would cry; they'd heard the story of what happened to the first grader. But after a while of Porter being consistently nice, some of the younger kids started saying hello back.

One day, Porter asked Beckett to come over to his house. He told Beckett, "My parents want to meet the kid who helped me finally like it here."

When Beckett visited Porter's house, Porter's parents were really nice to him. They told Beckett how bad they felt about having to move, especially when Porter's team was going to the championship, but they didn't have a choice.

His mom said, "We are so grateful you were kind to Porter. His behavior completely changed when we moved here. He used to be such a happy, fun and active kid. But when we moved, he moped around the house and wouldn't talk to us. We felt helpless and didn't know what to do to make things better for him."

Porter's dad added, "The day that you and Porter met with Mrs. Gables, he came home excited about the football game he had just played with you and your friends. He told us he had not been nice to kids at school and was thought of as a bully. We were surprised that he was that mean. At his last school, he got in trouble for fighting a couple of times, but we always thought it was the other kid's fault. Now we realize he probably had something to do with it. We really appreciate that you didn't hold Porter's bad behavior against him and that you gave him a second chance."

Beckett said, "My mom told me Porter may have been acting that way because he wasn't happy. But I didn't believe her until I talked to Porter that day. When I heard how upset he was about missing the championship game, I felt really bad for him. I'd be upset, too. I'm happy the football coaches allowed him to help out at practice. And we all love playing football with him because he has such an awesome arm."

Chapter

8

Porter was feeling better about being at Rock Hill Elementary and really appreciated how nice everyone was to him even though he had been such a jerk. One day, he said to Beckett, "I guess it's cool to be nice to people."

That got Beckett thinking. What if everyone knew it was cool to be nice? Wouldn't the world be a better place if people were kind to one another? So he came up with the idea of starting a club and enlisted Tony, Dan and Porter to help. They met during recess and lunch to discuss what they would do in the club.

"So what's this club for?" Porter asked.

"You said the other day that it's cool to be nice. It made me think about the saying – It's Cool to Be Kind. Wouldn't it be cool to get kids at school to be kinder to each other? We could give kids something for being kind. What do you guys think it should be?" Beckett said.

"We could give out stickers. Most kids love stickers, especially the girls," Dan suggested.

"Dudes, we should make a cool logo for our club that we can put on the stickers," said Tony.

The boys made posters of examples of kind acts to be posted around the school and worked on drawings of their logo. They decided to name the club the "Cool to Be Kind Movement" because they wanted to start a movement to spread kindness around the world. They all worked really hard on the logo. When it was finished, they were all excited!

"Do you really think kindness could spread all over the world? Wouldn't that be amazing?" Porter asked. When he said that, Beckett thought to himself, Wow! The meanest kid I've ever met now wants to spread kindness around the world. Now that was cool!

COOL TO BE

KIND MOVEMENT

The Cool to Be Kind Movement Club members met with Mrs. Gables and their principal, Mrs. Lynn, to share their idea.

"We created a club, and our goal is to encourage kids to be kind to one another. We named the club the Cool to Be Kind Movement because we want to start a movement to spread kindness all over the world. We want to give out stickers to kids who are seen being kind," Beckett said.

Mrs. Lynn loved the idea and asked, "What can the school do to help?"

Mrs. Gables suggested, "We could have posters up in the cafeteria listing different kids' kind acts. That way, they could see them and show them off to their friends. We could hold assemblies each month highlighting some of the kids who were kind. But first, we need to have an assembly to explain what the club is about and your goal of spreading kindness in the school and then all over the world. That is a big goal, but I'm proud of you for striving for it."

Beckett, Tony, Dan and Porter prepared their speeches for the assembly. They were all nervous about talking in front of the entire school.

Porter was especially nervous because he knew that there were probably some kids who still thought he was mean. Dan felt like puking every time he thought about getting up on stage to speak.

At the assembly, Beckett started by saying, "We created a club that focuses on how important it is to be kind. It's called the Cool to Be Kind Movement. When you are kind to someone, it not only makes that person feel good but you also feel good. And kindness can do even more. Treating a person with kindness can change a person's attitude and behavior. Look at what happened with Porter."

Every student in the cafeteria was listening intently because they still didn't understand why Porter had changed and why Beckett was now friends with him. Beckett motioned for Porter to come to the front to speak. Porter cleared his throat and began his speech.

"I was so unhappy when I came to this school because I didn't want to move here. I wanted to stay home and play on my football team that's now going to the championship. I was mad at my parents and at everyone else that I was stuck here. So when I came to this school, I took it out on anyone who got in my way. I was mean to every kid I passed in the hallway. I feel really badly about it now. I wish I had come in with a better attitude. When Beckett heard about my situation, he understood that I had a reason to be upset. He told me that my reaction made the situation even worse. Even though I had threatened to knock Beckett out, he still asked me to help with his football team and to play football with his friends after school. He made me feel welcome here – like I could actually belong here. I have seen how an act of kindness can change how someone sees the world. Beckett did that for me. Now I like it here. I hope that you guys can all forgive me for how mean I was and give me a second chance."

All of the kids in the cafeteria clapped after Porter spoke. They were impressed that Beckett's kindness could transform Porter into someone as nice as he seemed during his speech! Tony walked up to the podium.

"We will be rewarding your kind acts by giving out Cool to Be Kind Movement stickers. We called it the Cool to Be Kind Movement because we want to spread kindness not just around our school but also around the world. Wouldn't that be cool to be a part of a movement that spreads kindness around the world?"

The students all nodded and looked at each other excitedly. Kindness spreading around the world. Wow. That would be amazing!

Beckett glanced over and saw that Dan's face was green. He patted Dan on the back and whispered, "You've got this buddy."

Dan had been hiding at the back of the stage. Even though he was afraid he might pass out, Dan bravely walked up to the podium. With his hair hanging down his face and his eyes peeking out, he explained more about the club.

"Not only will we be handing out stickers, but we will also have posters up in the cafeteria where your kind acts will be described for the entire school to see. And each month, kind kids will be nominated to receive a special award at a monthly Cool to Be Kind Movement assembly. The kind kids will be brought on stage to explain their kind acts and will be applauded for their kindness."

The kids were all so excited about the idea of being recognized for being kind. They couldn't wait until Monday when the Cool to Be Kind Movement was starting in their school.

In fact, they didn't even wait. Kids started being kinder to each other right away!

Chapter

9

On Monday, the Cool to Be Kind Movement Club members got to school early. They were ready to hang the posters, listing the types of kind things people could do. Beckett, Tony, Dan and Porter thought that the students would be kind but had no idea how much the Cool to Be Kind Movement would change their school.

COOL TO BE

KIND MOVEMENT

1. Help a student or teacher.

2. Say something nice to someone.

3. Invite a student to play a game with you.

4. Hold the door for someone.

5. Talk to a student who looks sad or upset and ask if they are okay.

Kind Kids were everywhere! Kids were proud to show off the stickers on their backpacks and lunchboxes. So many stickers were given out that Beckett had to print more every day. Kids loved going to school and finding new ways to be kind. The teachers and the school staff even got involved.

One day, they were able to put up over 50 Kind Kids acts on the posters in the cafeteria! Some of the acts were as simple as helping someone with a difficult math problem or hugging someone who was crying.

But what surprised the club members the most was the kind acts the kids were doing outside of the school.

KIND ACTS

1. Gary T. went to school early to help his teacher prepare for a science experiment.

2. Brady G. brought in school supplies for a friend who didn't have any at home.

3. Hailey H. stood up for a friend who was being bullied at recess.

4. Kerry M. helped a friend on crutches get to her classroom.

5. Jaiden S. helped a boy pick up his tray when he dropped it in the cafeteria and got him another lunch.

One day, a third grader named Bryan approached Beckett to tell him about his kind act. "I was worried about my best friend who lives next door," Bryan said. "He always seemed so hungry every time he came over to play. I asked him what he ate for dinner, and he told me that they don't eat dinner every night because they didn't have enough money for food. It made me feel sad so I told my mom. She was sad too and told me we needed to help. My mom asked our other neighbors to bring meals and extra groceries to the family on different nights.

"Beckett, you should have seen my friend's mom's face when we brought over the first meal and groceries. She cried and told my mom how bad she felt about not having enough money for food. She said now she could feed her children and have enough money to pay for rent so they don't get kicked out on the streets." Bryan beamed as he shared his story.

Beckett smiled widely. "Bryan, your kind act has made such a difference in your friend's life. You should be proud of yourself."

Bryan said, "Helping my friend felt so good. Now all I want to do is find more people to help."

Chapter

10

After a couple of months, Mrs. Lynn and Mrs. Gables called the Cool to Be Kind Movement members into the office for a meeting.

"Do you think they are going to stop the club?" Dan whispered to Beckett as they walked to the office.

"I doubt it," Beckett answered. "But I have no idea why they want to meet."

"Hi boys, come on in," said Mrs. Lynn. "I have been getting calls from a lot of parents about your club." The boys glanced at each other thinking maybe parents didn't like their club. Mrs. Lynn smiled.

"It's nothing to worry about. Actually, parents are thrilled about how the Cool to Be Kind Movement has inspired their children to be kind at home and to people in the community."

Mrs. Gables added, "In fact, one of the parents works at the local news station and wants to do a story on your club."

Tony got up and danced a little gig. "That is so awesome!! I'm going to be on TV!" Then he high fived everyone, including Mrs. Lynn. They all laughed. Beckett looked over at Dan wondering how he felt about being on TV. Dan's face was bright red, and he was wringing his hands.

"You only have to talk if you feel comfortable," Mrs. Gables said also noticing Dan's reaction. Dan let out a deep breath and smiled.

The following week, the TV crew showed up, interviewed the club members, and followed them around the school. They videotaped all of the kind acts happening at school. They showed the stickers on the kids' backpacks and lunch boxes and the poster of the kids' kind acts.

The show was such a hit that the station started listing Kind Kids Acts every night on its 5:30 p.m. news show. Other news stations picked up the story, and soon, the Cool to Be Kind Movement club members were asked to speak at another elementary school in their school district.

"Are you sure this is a good idea?" Dan asked the group. "You know Clyde goes there, and he is one tough kid. He is definitely going to make fun of our club."

"Who's Clyde?" Porter asked.

"We play his football team, and they kill us every year. Clyde is one big and scary dude," Tony answered.

"But if we want to spread our movement of being kind around the world, we need to tell other schools about it," Beckett said even though he secretly agreed with Dan and Tony.

The day of the presentation at the elementary school, all of the boys except Porter were really nervous. He had never met the boys on the other football team so he didn't know what to expect. As they walked up on the stage, they were booed loudly.

"Man, these guys are such losers. What a stupid name for a club!" yelled a really big kid. Beckett looked over and realized it was Clyde. He saw the principal stand up and give the kids a look, which made them stop booing.

Beckett took a deep breath and kept walking on the stage. Dan had almost run away when he heard the booing, but he didn't want his friends to have to face this tough crowd by themselves. Instead, he quickly hid behind his friends and positioned himself closest to the door in case he had to make a fast getaway.

Porter told Beckett that he wanted to speak first. He addressed the angry kids.

"I get it that you guys think a club about kindness is lame." He pointed to Beckett, "But Beckett's kindness helped me change my attitude about how much I hated it at my new school. My parents made me move here. I had to stop playing football and miss going to the championship with my team. I was really mad, and I took it out on almost everyone I passed in the hallway. Kids at my school thought I was a bully. I even threatened to knock Beckett out. But he listened to my situation and helped me. He talked to his football coach, and now I help out at their practice. He even invited me to play football with his friends after school."

When Porter was done speaking, Beckett decided to talk directly to Clyde.

"Hey Clyde," Beckett said, "we play football against each other."

"I know, and we always beat you," Clyde snickered, and the kids in the audience laughed.

"That's true. Your team is really good. My name is Beckett. I hope you'll give us a chance to speak and explain our club. So I was wondering – has anyone ever done anything nice for you that made you feel really good?"

At first, Clyde looked like he was going to make fun of Beckett. But then, he stopped.

"You know what – someone has done something nice for me. My basketball coach goes out of his way to make sure I get to practice. My parents both work two jobs and can't take me. He picks me up and takes me to practice. After practice, he stops by his house to pick up the dinner that his wife made for me and my sister because she knows that my mom is at her second job and isn't home to make us dinner."

"How do you feel when your coach takes you to practice and his wife makes you and your sister dinner?" Beckett asked.

"Really happy and relieved that I don't have to make dinner," Clyde responded.

"Your coach is really cool because of how kind he is to you. All we're saying is that it makes people feel good to have someone do something nice for them. If you do something kind for someone, you could make them feel as good as your coach makes you feel. That's what we want to spread around the world, being kind to others and making people feel good."

Clyde nodded. He finally got why the club wasn't lame. He stood up and said to the other students at his school, "Let's listen to these kids. I like their idea of being kind. We could use some of that here at our school."

Beckett and his friends were able to give their presentations without any more booing and even got a standing ovation at the end!

Pretty soon, there were Cool to Be Kind Movement clubs in all of the schools in their state! After the movement spread across Pennsylvania, they were asked to be interviewed on a national news station. This was huge! Now there was a chance that the Cool to Be Kind Movement could spread across the entire country. Beckett and his friends were beside themselves with excitement!

Since things were getting much bigger than they ever imagined, the club members decided to create a Cool to Be Kind Movement website so kids from all over the country could write about their Kind Acts. They asked the computer teacher, Mr. Burch, to help them set it up. The Kind Acts were posted on the website. People could order stickers and posters from the website. Kind kids were also encouraged to make their own logos and send them in to be seen by all the Cool to Be Kind Movement members around the country.

Even Clyde submitted his story to the website. He wrote about how he created a Cool to Be Kind Movement club at his school. His club started a fundraiser to raise money to help kids in his area who weren't able to play sports because they couldn't afford to pay for their sporting equipment or the fees to join the team. So far, his club has helped ten kids join different teams!

One of the kind acts posted on the website was extremely touching. A sixth grader named Sandra from Oregon wrote in that she had always been embarrassed because her parents could never afford to buy her the expensive shoes all the kids were wearing. She felt like she never really fit in. But the Cool to Be Kind Movement opened her eyes that it isn't the clothes or shoes you wear that make you cool. You can be cool just by being kind.

COOL TO BE

KIND MOVEMENT

www.cooltobekindmovement.com

1. Kaitlyn F. from Wisconsin collected food for her local food bank.

2. Casey H. from Texas organized a group of kids to have lemonade stands and donated the money to the American Cancer Society.

3. Sarah T. from Ohio created a Cool to Be Kind Movement Club at her school and they went to local nursing homes and played cards with the people living there.

4. Jordan G. from Arizona gathered backpacks and toys for kids in a homeless shelter.

5. Aiden B. from California collected supplies for animals at a local animal shelter.

One day, when Sandra was watching television, she saw a story about children in Africa who walk around barefoot because they don't own shoes. This story inspired her to do something. She put out flyers in her school and community requesting shoes for the Cool to Be Kind Movement. Sandra collected over one thousand pairs of shoes and had a teacher help her send them to the kids in Africa who were in the story she saw on television. She even included Cool to Be Kind Movement stickers for the kids.

Rock Hill Elementary School held a Cool to Be Kind Movement assembly to share the news that their movement had spread to Africa.

Beckett proudly announced, "We did it! The Cool to Be Kind Movement is now global!" The students gave a standing ovation to the club members.

As the year went on, Beckett and the other club members invited younger students to join the club so that it would continue when they went on to middle school. When they started middle school, Beckett and his friends met with the guidance counselor and principal and started a club there, too. Will you start one at your school, too?

What can YOU do today that is kind?

KINDNESS CAN CHANGE THE WORLD.

Dear Readers,

Hello! I'm so excited that you've read this book. Who was your favorite character?

The goal of this book is to help readers understand how being kind can help in different situations and how one act of kindness can spread and create even more kind acts. The book also teaches you how you can control your reaction to an event and that your reaction affects the outcome (Event + Response = Outcome or E + R = O).

You can be a part of the Cool to Be Kind Movement! Just send an email to

linneamcfadden@cooltobekindmovement.com. You or your parents can write in your kind acts, which will be posted on the website. Then check out our website: www.cooltobekindmovement.com to see your kind act! If you want a Cool to Be Kind Movement club to start in your school, include the name of your school and the name of your principal or guidance counselor in your email to linneamcfadden@cooltobekindmovement.com.

Bullying

In the book, Beckett was able to approach Porter with the help of his guidance counselor, and their issue was resolved pretty quickly. I realize that this may not happen in real life and that you or someone you know may be dealing with something much worse. If that is the case, I want you to know that it is very important to talk to an adult –

a parent, a family member, a teacher, a guidance counselor, a coach, anyone. In any situation of bullying, it is important to tell someone even if you don't think they would think it was serious. Being mistreated is not okay. Even minor teasing doesn't feel good – believe me, I know. I had to wear a patch on my right eye when I was young, which made first grade the worst year for me. It is okay if your parents have to go into the school to talk to a teacher or principal about it. The most important thing is that the bullying stops.

Girls

This book is focused on boys, but it doesn't mean that bullying doesn't happen with girls. If you are being mistreated by a girl (even by someone you consider a friend), please tell an adult. And check out the book series *Dork Diaries*. The author started the series because of the way her daughter was treated at school.

My Secret Bully is another good book about how girls can be mean and was written because the author's daughter was being mistreated by her close friend. The books are listed in the kids' resources section under Girl Books.

Cyberbullying

Cyberbullying is a new way that kids and even adults have started bullying. People are being mean on social media, including Kik, ooVo, Yik Yak, Facebook, Instagram, Twitter, Snapchat as well as through texting. If you experience bullying online, you need to tell an adult. Tell as many adults as necessary until someone does something to help you.

Dear Parents,

I hope you and your child enjoyed this book and that your child is inspired to do kind things. Readers can email linneamcfadden@cooltobekindmovement.com. The kind acts will be listed on the website with first name, last initial, and state. You are welcome to send in a picture as well. In addition, Kind Kids acts will be listed on the Cool to Be Kind Movement Facebook, Instagram and Twitter accounts.

Bullying

I purposely made the bullying situation easily fixable because the focus of this book is to empower kids and to teach kindness. I want kids to understand that they have the power to control how they respond to different situations and that their response can change the outcome. I also wanted to show that sometimes kids with bad behaviors aren't necessarily bad kids.

Certainly, there are cases of bullying that are much more severe. Bullying is rampant in some schools and can make life unbearable for kids. It is such a sad thing for a child to be treated terribly by his peers. In my letter to the readers, I stated that if they are being mistreated by anyone they should tell an adult. It is okay for parents to contact the school about the situation. I have done that myself for situations that have happened with my children in school. And with my children, I learned that even minor teasing can make them not want to go to school.

About Girls

This book is focused on boys because I wanted to reach a bigger audience. Boys would be less likely to read a book just about girls. Also the type of bullying girls experience is much different. If your daughter is experiencing any type of negative situation with girls, the book *Little Girls Can Be Mean: Four Steps to Bully-proof Girls in the Early Grades* is very informative and gives steps on how to help your daughter. It helped me when my daughter was going through tough situations with her friends. The book is listed in the Resources section.

Cyberbullying

Unfortunately, more and more children and adults are being bullied via social media each day. Since the person doing the bullying is behind a computer or a smart phone, the things that are said may be even crueler than what is said to someone's face. If your child is being bullied online, it is extremely important to intervene by calling the school and involving the police if necessary.

Kids Resources

Bullying Picture Books

The Juice Box Bully by Bob Sornson
and Maria Dismondy
Just Kidding by Trudy Ludwig
The Invisible Boy by Trudy Ludwig
Better Than You by Trudy Ludwig
Confessions of a Former Bully by
Trudy Ludwig
One by Kathryn Otoshi
The Recess Queen by Alexis O'Neill
Teasing isn't Funny by Melissa Higgins
Smallest Girl in the Smallest Grade by
Justin Roberts

Bullying Chapter Books

Wonder by R.J. Palacio
Auggie and Me by R.J. Palacio
Because of Mr. Terupt by Rob Buyea

Schooled by Gordon Korman

Kindness Books – Kids

Kids Random Acts of Kindness by The Editors of Conari Press
Kindness Is Cooler, Mrs. Ruler by Margery Cuyler and Sachiko Yoshikawa
How Full Is Your Bucket? For Kids by Tom Rath and Mary Reckmeyer
One Smile by Cindy McKinley
Each Kindness by Jacqueline Woodson
Quite the Same by Annette Garber

Girl Books

Dork Diaries by Rachel Renée Russell
My Secret Bully by Trudy Ludwig
Trouble Talk by Trudy Ludwig
Bully by Patricia Polacco

Parent/Teacher Resources

Event + Response = Outcome

The Success Principles, 10th Anniversary Edition by Jack Canfield

Bullying books

Bullying Epidemic: Not Just Child's Play by Lorna Blumen
Little Girls Can Be Mean: Four Steps to Bully-proof Girls in the Early Grades by Michelle Anthony and Reyna Lindert
The Survival Guide to Bullying: Written by a Teen by Aija Mayrock
Bully: An Action Plan for Teachers, Parents and Communities to Combat the Bullying Crisis by Lee Hirsch and Cynthia Lowen
Dear Bully edited by Megan Hall and Carrie Jones

Please Stop Laughing at Me... One Woman's Inspirational Story by Jodee Blanco

Please Stop Laughing at Us... by Jodee Blanco

Bullied Kids Speak Out... We Survived - How You Can Too by Jodee Blanco

Bullying Websites

www.thebullyproject.com
www.cyberbullying.org
www.stopbullying.gov
www.bullyingepidemic.com
www.pacerkidsagainstbullying.com
www.stompoutbullying.org

Documentaries

Bully by Lee Hirsch and Cynthia Lowen - a film following children who are bullied. This is powerful and should be shown to middle school children only.

Kindness is Contagious – Catherine
Ryan Hyde and David Gaz
Inspire Hope by Bryon Evans and Brian
Williams

Kindness Books – Adults

*Am I Being Kind: How Asking One
Simple Question Can Change Your
Life ... and Your World* by Michael J.
Chase
*Invisible Acts of Power: Channeling
Grace in Your Everyday Life* by
Carolyn Myss
Chicken Soup for the Soul by Jack
Canfield and Mark Victor Hansen
*The Power of Kindness: The
Unexpected Benefits of Leading a
Compassionate Life* by Piero Ferrucci
and Dalai Lama
The Kindness Diaries by Leon
Logothetis

Why Kindness is Good For You by David Hamilton

The Five Side Effects of Kindness by David Hamilton

Kindness Boomerang: How to Save the World (And Yourself) Through 365 Acts by Orly Wahba

Kindness Websites

www.randomactsofkindness.org
www.positive-focus.com
www.lifereimagined.com
www.livehappy.com
www.lifevestinside.com
www.thinkkindness.org
www.spreadkindness.org

ABOUT THE AUTHOR

Linnea McFadden has a Master's in Social Work from the University of Georgia. She has worked with children and families in child abuse prevention programs, homeless shelters and foster care, and as a behavioral specialist with autistic children. She currently works part-time in the research department of PinnacleCare, a healthcare advisory company, and resides in Pennsylvania with her husband and two children. This is her first children's book.

www.cooltobekindmovement.com
www.linneamcfadden.com

Author photo: Rachel Hudgins Photography

Made in the USA
Columbia, SC
21 January 2018